DATE DUE

APR 1 3 2012		
SEP 1 8 2012		
OCT 2 3 2012	MAR 2 9 2016	
OCT 2 3 2013		
NOV 3 0 2015		
NOV 3 0 2015		
NOV 3 0 2015		
FEB 0 6 2017		

DRAGONBLOOD

WINGS ABOVE THE WAVES

BY MICHAEL DAHL

ILLUSTRATED BY
FEDERICO PIATTI

STONE ARCH BOOKS
a capstone imprint

Zone Books are published by
Stone Arch Books
A Capstone Imprint
151 Good Counsel Drive, P.O. Box 669
Mankato, Minnesota 56002
www.capstonepub.com

Library of Congress Cataloging-in-Publication Data is
available on the Library of Congress website.

Library Binding: 978-1-4342-1924-4

Art Director: Kay Fraser
Graphic Designer: Hilary Wacholz
Production Specialist: Michelle Biedscheid

TABLE OF CONTENTS

CHAPTER 1
THE RESCUE 5

CHAPTER 2
THE SEA MONSTER 14

CHAPTER 3
MONSTER DREAMS 21

CHAPTER 4
THE HAUL 29

Introduction

A new Age of Dragons is about to begin. The powerful creatures will return to rule the world once more, but this time will be different. This time, they will have allies. Who will help them? Around the world, some young humans are making a strange discovery. They are learning that they were born with dragon blood – blood that gives them amazing powers.

CHAPTER 1
THE RESCUE

Off the coast of Brazil, a fishing boat rocked on the waves.

A **Storm** had passed over the sea during the night. Finally, the sky had cleared, but the **waves** were still rough.

Carlos **worked** on the fishing boat with his father and uncle.

Day after day they would **CAST** their nets for fish. It was hard work.

This morning, Carlos saw a shadow **bobbing** up and down on the waves.

"Look over there!" he shouted.

A woman was **drifting** in the sea.

She was holding on to a piece of **wood** that floated on the water.

The fishing boat drew near the **floating** woman.

Carlos and his uncle helped **pull** the woman onto the deck.

They **COVERED** her shoulders with a blanket.

Carlos gave her a cup of **hot** coffee to drink.

"Were you caught in the storm last night?" asked Carlos's father.

The woman shook her head and **shivered.**

"It was NOT the storm," she said.

"It was a **MONSTER.**"

CHAPTER 2
THE SEA MONSTER

"We saw a shadow in the night sky," said the woman.

"Somebody said it was a sea monster, but I did not believe them," the woman said.

"Then I saw something flying toward our ship."

"I watched it fly past the moon," she said.

"It looked as if it was having trouble flying. As if it did not know how to use its wings."

"I thought I was going crazy," said the woman.

"That's when the creature crashed into our boat. And then the storm came. My friends were lost at sea."

"Thank you for rescuing me," she said, quietly.

Then the woman **STARED** at Carlos. She was looking at his arm.

Carlos felt nervous. The woman was staring at his **BIRTHMARK**.

It was **shaped** like a dragon.

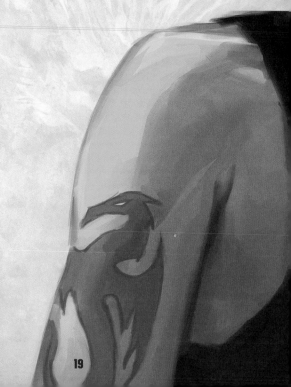

"The **monster!**" cried the woman.

She stood and *pointed* at Carlos's arm.

"That is what the monster looked like," she said.

Then she tried to **jump** off the boat.

CHAPTER 3

MONSTER DREAMS

Carlos's father and uncle **held** on to the woman.

"I must get off this boat!" she cried.

The two older men tried to calm her down.

They led her down some steps to the boat's cabin.

Carlos **stayed** up on deck. He heard his father telling the woman that she must rest.

"We must try to find your friends," his father said. "Then we will return to shore."

While the woman stayed in the cabin, the men searched the waves.

They decided **NOT** to haul for fish that day. But they did not see anyone else floating in the water.

That night, Carlos slept on deck.

The woman's shouts had bothered him. They seemed to become part of his dreams.

In one dream, Carlos grew great
WINGS.

He soared into the *windy* sky.

He saw his shadow below him
in the moonlight.

The shadow *glided* across the
water. It was shaped like his
birthmark. It was a **HUGE** and
graceful dragon.

The dragon darted back and forth across the **WATER**.

Its **claws** dipped into the waves, pulling up fish after fish.

And then Carlos's dream **drifted** away.

CHAPTER 4
THE HAUL

The blackness of the sky was becoming dark blue. The sun would soon rise **above** the waves.

Carlos could hardly move. His arms and legs felt **HEAVY**.

His hair was **dripping** with sweat.

Carlos heard shouts. He wearily opened his eyes.

His father and uncle were standing on deck. They were pointing and SHOUTING.

The woman they had rescued joined them on deck. Her eyes grew wide with **amazement**.

"Philip! Juan! Lisa!" she cried. "You're all right."

Carlos looked around him.

Three strangers lying on the deck were waking up. These were the woman's friends.

Carlos closed his eyes again. He felt as if he had been hauling fish all night long.

Sea Monster Mysteries

Do sea monsters really exist? Throughout history, there have been legends and stories and myths that tell of mysterious beasts roaming the oceans and lakes.

The Loch Ness Monster, or Nessie, is the most well known sea creature in the world. Stories about Nessie have been circulating since 1933. About 4,000 sightings have been reported.

The study of unknown species is called **cryptozoology**. It describes the search for legendary animals like the Loch Ness monster, Sasquatch, the Yeti, and many others.

Champ, the sea monster of Lake Champlain, Vermont, was first reported in 1819. It is known as America's Loch Ness monster. It has been seen about 300 times.

In 1908, the sea legend of Manipogo surfaced. This creature was spotted in Lake Manitoba in Canada. It is said to look like a large black snake or eel.

The **Kraken** was one of the scariest sea creatures known to sailors. The Kraken was a huge sea creature that could crush a ship with just one tentacle. It was supposed to live off the coast of Norway. Scientists believe that the Kraken's legend was actually based on a giant squid.

ABOUT THE AUTHOR

Michael Dahl is the author of more than 200 books for children and young adults. He has won the AEP Distinguished Achievement Award three times for his nonfiction. His Finnegan Zwake mystery series was shortlisted twice by the Anthony and Agatha awards. He has also written the Library of Doom series. He is a featured speaker at conferences around the country on graphic novels and high-interest books for boys.

ABOUT THE ILLUSTRATOR

After getting a graphic design degree and working as a designer for a couple of years, Federico Piatti realized he was spending way too much time drawing and painting, and too much money on art books and comics, so his path took a turn toward illustration. He currently works creating imagery for books and games, mostly in the fantasy and horror genres. Argentinian by birth, he now lives in Madrid, Spain, with his wife, who is also an illustrator.

GLOSSARY

birthmark (BURTH-mark)—a mark on the skin that was there from birth

bobbing (BOB-ing)—moving up and down in the water

cabin (KAB-in)—a private room on a ship for passengers to sleep in

cast (KAST)—to throw a fishing net into the water

creature (KREE-chur)—a living being

drifting (DRIFT-ing)—moving with the water

haul (HAWL)—to pull something out of the water

rough (RUHF)—not smooth

wearily (WIHR-uh-lee)—tiredly

DISCUSSION QUESTIONS

1. What **happened** to Philip, Lisa, and Juan? How did they get onto Carlos's boat?

2. Why was the woman **afraid** of Carlos?

3. How did Carlos feel about his **BIRTHMARK?** Explain your answer.

WRITING PROMPTS

1. Tell this story from **Philip's** point of view. What happens to him? How does he feel? What does he see and hear?

2. Pretend you're Carlos. Write a **letter** home to your mother about your time on the boat.

3. Carlos and his father **haul** fish together. Write about something you do with a family member.

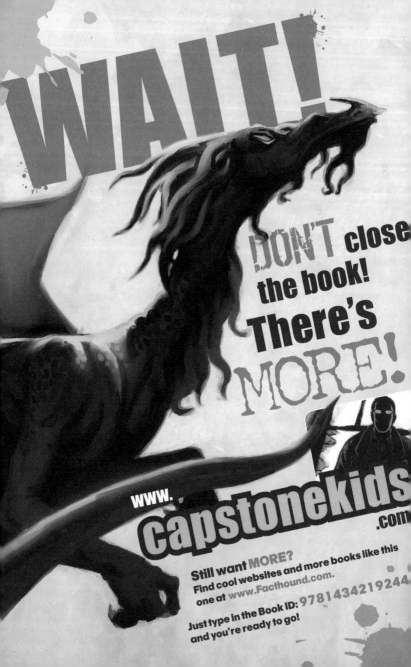